Prolance

www.prolancewriting.com
California, USA
©2020 Ali H. Chemkhi

ISBN: 978-1-7345760-7-8

Assmaa A. Andulsi
The Girl Who is Like No Other
Based on a Real Girl!

Ali H. Chemkhi

Cover art by Lamya Sharaby

PROLANCE

Dedication

To my mother Mariam.
She taught me to never give up.

To my father Hasan.
He taught me the art of storytelling.

To my wife Zina.
She kept reminding me about my potential.

To my four kids Asma, Shaima, Ahmad and Yomna.
They gave me the chance to live and share great
memorable moments with them.

To all my teachers.
They believed in my writing skills.

To my friends Dr. Dany Doueiri and Judy Hamrouni.
They helped editing this book with love.

Table of Contents

Chapter One
The Girl Who is Like No Other

I am Assmaa A. Andulsi, the girl who is like no other.

Now, when you look at me, you might not notice too many things that are different about me. I am really skinny and tall, but so are many girls my age. My skin is a pretty tan color, so sometimes people greet me by saying "Hola!" in Spanish. I was born with a bouquet of dark hair that made me look like a doll. Now my long hair is as shiny as a raven's wing. I also let my thin eyebrows meet in the middle for good luck!

None of that really matters, though. That is just how I look. You have to know me a little more to see what a unique girl I really am. I tell my very best friend Christa that I should be more famous than Snow White, Princess Aurora or Cinderella. Christa is of Mexican origins and has short, light brown hair that curls in the cutest way. She likes to wear skinny jeans and nice shirts, and she always makes me laugh. And I make her laugh too when I tell her how famous I should be.

"You might be famous someday but not today!" she says.

I, Assmaa A. Andulsi, really am a girl like no other. Just look at my name. The last two letters of my first name leave no doubt that I am a girl from either Arab, French, English or Spanish descent. The two s's serve as an honest warning that my name is not asthma! Some of my teachers and friends pronounce my name that way the first time they meet me. But the first part is pronounced ah. That is easy to remember because whenever we are happy with something, we say, "Ah, what a delicious piece of cake!" So thank you, Mama, for the two a's and the two s's!

The middle initial stands for Amer, which is my Dad's name. That means my initials are AAA, just like the batteries.

Christa often says, "You are tiny and skinny like triple A batteries anyway."

"So when I grow up I will be big and fat like double A batteries!" I say.

Andulsi, my last but not least name, means somebody who comes from Andalusia. That country used to exist in Spain some hundred years ago. My great-great-grandfather moved from there to settle in the country of Tunisia. So of course my father is from Tunisia in North Africa. In Tunisia they speak French as a second language to Arabic.

"You are the second translation," Papa says.

Whenever he says that, I know he is talking about my last name. There is an "i" at the end of my last name, and some people think that makes me Italian. But that letter was meant to be the French version for Tunisia. Then we had to move again and translate it into English. The original Arabic letter should have become an "e" but instead the translation went from French to English. So here I am with an "i". That is what I get for wearing so many hats with so many different colors, shapes and flavors!

Mama always says, "I hope there will be

no third translation!"

So, all that moving around by my great-great-grandfather and my father means I am African-American but I am not black. I am originally from Spain but I do not speak Spanish. I am a Muslim but I go to a mosque that stands high upon the shores of the Pacific Ocean.

I, Assmaa A. Andulsi, carry with me two bags stuffed with the two versions of me. One speaks English and the other speaks Arabic. At my regular school I learn how to read and write from left to right. At my weekend school, I learn how to read and write from right to left. My weekend school is next door to the mosque, where my family worships. It is really just a trailer but it is decorated beautifully inside and very comfortable. There I learn Islamic history, read from the religious book called the Qur'an, hear about the Prophet Mohamed's traditions, and learn Islamic manners.

So really I am learning things from two different worlds. I blend them together every day. Although sometimes at home, I forget which assignment I'm working on. Then I discover I have been writing Arabic when I should have been writing English or the other way around. Whenever that happens, I laugh so hard I cry!

I learn a lot of English words from my parents. At the same time, I laugh when their accents make the words come out sounding funny. Then I laugh at myself because sometimes I get mixed up between the two languages when I talk. Some of my words come out in English, while others come out in Arabic. My Mom has special words for when that happens.

"Sometimes you speak Englic, and sometimes you speak Arabish," she says with a smile.

"One day I will invent a new language," I say.

"What will you call it?" she asks.

"How about Aralish?" I joke.

Well, with all those things that are different, you can see why I am a girl who is like no other. Christa does not let me go too far with that idea, though.

"I am still not convinced," she says.

"I told you all the things that make me different," I say.

"But different like no other? That is hard

to believe," she says.

"Well, then, I beg your pardon. Just remember that I am only eight years old!" I say.

She laughs. "So, are there any other special things I should know about the girl who is like no other?"

"Just imagine me when I turn eighteen and walk downtown wearing blue jeans with a long green blouse and a pink scarf wrapped around my head. I will hold a flag with fifty stars and red and white stripes chanting 'Long live freedom!' Then you can ask for more reasons why I am a girl who is like no other!"

Chapter Two
My Grandfather was a King

I knew all about those things that make me like no other girl for a long time. Then one day my Dad surprised me with something new.

"You, Assmaa A. Andulsi, could be called a princess," he said.

"A real princess?" I asked.

"Well, maybe not a real princess. But some kind of princess!" he said.

Dad always says that when I am getting ready to go somewhere. He says I fuss over my clothes as much as a princess! Purple is my favorite color, so a lot of things in my closet are purple. I usually wear jeans with pretty designs on them.

I like to match them with simple shirts. Most of the time I know what jeans go with each shirt. On some days, though, I change clothes two or three times before I find an outfit I like.

Even though my Dad calls me a princess as a joke, I think I might be a real princess! If it is true then everyone will know right away that I, Assmaa A. Andulsi, am a girl who is like no other!

One day I was going through my Dad's journal. English is my favorite subject in school because we get to read and write stories and poems. My Dad writes all kinds of things in his journal. He writes about things we do as a family because he wants to remember the fun we have together.

On other days, he writes down ideas for new games we can play. He is always coming up with great ideas!

Every once in a while, he writes a poem. I really like reading those. I do not understand some of them but some of them are funny. Then one day I read a poem that said my grandfather was a king!

The first part of the poem read:

My father was a king,
I am not asking for his throne.
My father's kingdom was not a ring,
You pass it on when you step down.

Wow! You can guess how excited I was.

If my grandfather was a king then my father was, too. The daughter of a king is a princess. Since my Dad was a king, that made me a real princess! Even Christa would have to admit I really was like no other girl!

The next day I could not wait to tell my friends. The moment I arrived at school, I told the girl I walked down the sidewalk with that I was a princess. I told the boy who always holds the front door open for other people that I was a princess. On my way to my desk, I told my classmates I was a princess. Everyone at the cafeteria table where I ate lunch heard that I, Assmaa A. Andulsi, was a real, live princess!

By afternoon recess, everybody at school knew the history of my family. Christa and I always hang out during recess. Sometimes we play on the monkey bars. Everyone was talking about how my grandfather had been a king and that Assmaa A. Andulsi was a princess.

"Do princesses hang on monkey bars?" I asked Christa.

She just laughed. Then the bell rang. It was time to go back inside. We started up the curving pathway to the door. Some of the boys bowed to me. A few of the girls curtseyed! I told them they did not have to do that. But it was nice being a princess!

Christa wanted to make sure the teachers knew. Back in the classroom, she went right up to Mrs. Coffey, our third-grade teacher. Mrs. Coffey is short and skinny. I am almost as tall as she is! But her hair is blond and she wears glasses. I like her a lot because she is always so nice and calm. She is my favorite teacher ever...well, except maybe for my kindergarten teacher.

Christa asked, "Mrs. Coffey, do you know that we have a princess in our class?"

Mrs. Coffey smiled. "Who is that?" she asked.

"Assmaa! She is a princess. Her grandfather was a king!" Christa said.

"Oh, is that true, Assmaa?" Mrs. Coffey asked.

I nodded. Mrs. Coffey looked very surprised. She had probably never met a real princess before! Maybe she should have guessed it long ago. Purple is my favorite color, and purple is a royal color, so maybe I should have guessed it, too!

Before we knew what was happening, all my classmates stood up. Even though the room is really large, the desks are all sort of crowded together. So when everyone stood, it felt like I was in the middle of a big crowd! They started chanting,

"Little princess! Little princess!"

Well, Mrs. Coffey did not let that go on for too long. We were there to learn, and she quickly told us to settle down. She has always been a challenging teacher! That is part of why I like her so much. She helped me to learn how to study better.

The rest of the time in class was pretty quiet.

When the bell rang at the end of the day, I went out to wait for my Mom to pick me up. When I stepped through the school's front door, a bunch of students had lined up on the sidewalk. They gathered around me in a big crush.

"Can I have your autograph?" one boy

called.

"I want to have my picture taken with you!" a girl said.

"Me, too! Me, too!" they all shouted.

What a noisy, big crowd! Ms. Mumper, the principal, hurried up just then. Ms. Mumper has grey hair and tiny eyes hidden by a lot of wrinkles, but she is really nice. She always stands in front of the school to greet kids as they arrive each day. She stands outside again to say goodbye. But on this day, she had to find out who had started a rally on the sidewalk! Ms. Ramirez, her secretary, jogged along behind her.

"What is happening here?" Ms. Mumper yelled over the crowd.

"A princess! A real princess in our school!" Alex Walker shouted.

Alex is in my class. He is the tallest boy in school. He is kind of bossy and acts like he is allowed to speak for everybody. Maybe he does that because he hates his freckles. Or maybe it is because his ears are so big he always wears hats to cover them up. At any rate, he is kind of loud so he was really happy to break the news to the principal.

I, Assmaa A. Andulsi, was happy to be

the princess! It was exciting and delightful to be called princess. I felt really special, as if I were in my own Disney film. No, I felt more special. Disney characters are not real and I was a real, live princess!

Ms. Mumper adjusted her glasses. "Who in the world is a princess at our school?" she asked.

"Assmaa A. Andulsi," Adasena Brent said. "Her grandfather was a king."

Adasena is the only student who can speak faster and louder than Alex. She is African-American and always wears clothes that are in fashion. She is my second-best friend. Even though we like each other, we often get into arguments. We disagree on so many things. We just have different ways of doing things. So hearing her talk about me made me especially happy.

Ms. Mumper waved her hands. "I want everybody to hurry to their buses and the cars waiting to pick them up. Tomorrow you will all have a chance to meet the princess," she said.

All the kids scattered. Even though they had their hands full with their backpacks and homework and books, many waved at me one last time.

"Bye, Princess Assmaa!" they shouted.
I waved and smiled just like any princess would have done.

Chapter Three
Habibaty

Ms. Mumper did not give me a chance to sign a single autograph or even tell my friends goodbye. She held my hand and tugged me back to her office. Ms. Ramirez walked behind us carrying my backpack and the flowers my friends had given me during recess. Having someone carry my things made me feel proud. I, Assmaa A. Andulsi, was a real princess!

"Are you really a princess, Assmaa, or did you just make that up?" Ms. Mumper asked firmly.

"Yes, Ms. Mumper, I am a princess," I said.

"And you just discovered it today?" she asked.

"My Dad never told me anything about it," I said.

"So who told you?" she asked.

"Actually, I read it in my father notebook. He wrote that his father was a king," I said quietly.

I had thought that my friends might want to see the poem so I had copied my Dad's words. I dug through my things for the paper and handed it to her. "Here it is, Ms. Mumper," I said.

She took the paper then read it several times. "Your grandfather was a king without a throne," she read quietly.

"Hah, his kingdom was not a ring," she said a bit louder.

"The kingdom is passed along when the king steps down," she said even louder.

"Huh. This is a puzzle," she said.

After looking at her secretary, Ms. Mumper looked at me. "OK. I guess your Dad has to explain this puzzle. Is he picking you up today?" she asked.

"My Mom is picking me up," I said. Then I jumped up. "Oh no. I did not pick up my sister Aisha from her classroom! And I did not meet Mama at the door!"

"You were too busy with this princess thing," Ms. Mumper said.

"She must be waiting. It has been a long time!" I said.

Mama always worried so much about us kids. She was probably very upset. I needed to get to her fast! I grabbed my stuff and ran to Aisha's classroom. No one was there. The classroom had a lot of cute posters on the walls but I had never seen it totally empty before. It made me feel scared that something had happened to my sister. She usually waits for me to take her to the parents' parking lot where we meet Mama. She is only six and is too young to go by herself.

Poor Aisha. She must have been so frightened! I did not know what to do. Tears ran down my cheeks as I hurried back to my classroom then to Aisha's room again. She had disappeared! I finally went back to the principal's office.

"Ms. Ramirez, do you know where Aisha is?" I asked.

"I have not seen her, Honey" she said.

I ran to the front door of the school.

Mama usually waited for Aisha and me there. But she was not there, either! I looked around for her green van but did not see it in the parking lot. Icy fingers squeezed my stomach. Something had happened to Mama and Aisha! My tears fell like heavy rain on a winter day.

I threw the flowers to the ground. I threw my backpack on the sidewalk. Then I sat right down beside it. I was crying so hard I could not see. I had to think! I put my head between my hands and closed my eyes. Everything around me was so still and quiet at that moment. It felt calm, like being in Mrs. Coffey's quiet classroom. The first thought that came into my mind was a question.

Assmaa, what is better for you? Being a princess? Or being with your Mom and sister?

I did not have to think about the answer at all. I immediately spoke out loud to Allah. Allah is the Arabic name for God, so I knew my answer would be heard.

I said, "O Allah, I do not want to be a princess. Please bring my Mom and my sister back!"

At that very moment, Mom's hand touched my shoulder. Aisha was with her. My sister's chubby little body was shaking. She was laughing and crying at the same time. Her little girl's voice was so lovely!

"Assmaa, I was worried about you," Aisha said.

I grabbed her in a big hug. "I am sorry, habibaty," I said. Habibaty means darling in Arabic.

"Mama, I am very sorry," I kept repeating while hugging both of them and crying.

Habibaty was the word in my heart. I had been so worried about Aisha. To have her back was more important than anything else in my life!

On the way home, I thanked Allah for having answered my call so quickly. The puzzle about the king with no throne and me being a princess did not matter. I had made a deal with Allah. He had brought my Mom and my sister safely back to me. At the same time, He had taken the title of princess away from me.

I, Assmaa A. Andulsi, no longer cared about being a princess. The title was nothing more than a word. I had grown up watching movies about Cinderella, Snow White, and other princesses. It was supposed to be such a good thing but other things were much more important. I would never trade anyone in my family to be a princess.

After we got home, Mom told my Dad all about our day. He turned to me and looked at me for a long time. Then he asked me one question.

"Assmaa, would you still like to be a princess?" he asked.

"No, Daddy. I really do not want that," I mumbled.

That seemed to make him happy. He nodded and took out his journal. After turning to the poem, he pointed to the page.

"Assmaa, your grandfather was not the kind of king who had a throne, a gold ring or great power. He was a king because he took care of his family. He had eleven kids. He was never rich with gold and treasures. Instead he was rich with love and affection."

When he finished speaking, I looked up. My Dad had tears in his eyes.

"I am proud of you, Dad. You are my real king!" I said.

I jumped on him and hugged him as tightly as I could. After a lovely long minute, he pulled back and looked deep into my eyes.

"You have to tell your class the truth

about this," he said.

"Yes, Dad! I will be proud to tell them what the poem really means!" I said.

"You do not mind that I am not the kind of king who wears a crown?" he asked.

"Of course not! I will tell everyone all about you and what a real king is. You!" I said.

The very next morning, I marched right into class and asked Mrs. Coffey for permission to speak to the class. After I explained my mistake, I told them what a real king was. I told them how much my Dad cared about me and my brother and sister. When I was done, they burst into applause! They really did understand that my Dad was a real king...and not the kind that wore a crown.

Chapter Four
My Dad is a Dude

You now know that I love my family very much. I, Assmaa A. Andulsi, also love the Prophet Mohamed. He was the last Messenger sent by God to help people on this earth. Most of the kids in my school know about Jesus and Moses but some of them have never heard of Mohamed. He was so kind and so lovely! I can hear his words whispering in my ear saying, "All men are equal." And by "men," he meant both gentle ladies and gentlemen. These words blow my blood to my heart and my head. Every time I hear them, I am so happy I shiver!

I, Assmaa A. Andulsi, also love George Washington. He was the father of my country! He was a good man and very brave. He led the group that wrote the Constitution, and the Constitution also says all men are created equal! George Washington drove the British out of America. I imagine him after each battle struggling to raise the flag up high.

I, Assmaa A. Andulsi, admire Martin Luther King. He had a dream that changed history. He led a huge crowd of people on a march for civil rights. Then he gave a speech about keeping everyone in America free from hatred. He wanted all men to be equal! As I walk down the street, I can see how his dream came alive in America with my own eyes.

I, Assmaa A. Andulsi, also have a dream, a big one. I dream that one day people all over the world will be kind like the Prophet Mohamed. I dream that they will be brave like George Washington. And I dream that they will have a dream like Martin Luther King. But people do not have to be famous to be good. I have lots of people living in my house who do good things!

My Mom is very fashionable. She likes to dress in fancy styles. She puts all kinds of colorful clothes together to create pretty out-fits. She wears a scarf over her hair whenev-er she leaves the house. The scarf covers the beauty of her hair because Allah told women to be modest. To be modest is kind of like not bragging about something you are good at.

She spends a lot of time taking care of me and my sister and brother. She cooks a lot and we always gobble down whatever she makes. I really love her couscous! The meal looks simple. It is made with crushed wheat that is steamed. It is kind of like pasta only it is really light and fluffy. Mom adds spices and vegetables. I like it best when she adds lamb meat.

Mom also helps me out a lot. Whenever my homework is really tough, she sits down with me and helps me figure out the math problems. She also plays games with all of us kids. Sometimes I wish she did not watch over me so much, though. She wants me to learn how to be a good person so I do not always get to do what I want to do. But she gets me out of trouble all the time, so that is a good thing, too!

My Dad is also really great. He is pretty skinny like me but of course he is taller. He has a mustache and a thin beard. When he goes to work he wears suits but on the weekends he wears more comfortable clothes. He works hard but he still finds time for us kids. He takes me to the park on the weekends and tells us the best stories. He makes them up himself! Even when he is very tired after working all day, he still plays with us.

I, Assmaa A. Andulsi, dare to call my Dad "dude". That should not be a problem, right? After all, he is a dude. But in Arabic, that word means worm! Calling your Dad a worm is not a good idea. Sometimes I feel that speaking two different languages is painful. But he and I joke about that all the time. Whenever he comes home from work, I open the door for him.

"Hi, dude!" I say.

"Dude?" he asks. "I am not a worm!"

He laughs the whole time. I jump into his arms and wrap both arms around his neck. I kiss both his cheeks and between his eyes.

"You are so cute, dude!" I say.

My little brother Omar is always there to join in on the fun. Omar is not as tan as I am and his long, dark eyelashes stand out on his round face. He loves to ride his bike and play different sports...even if he is too young to know the rules!

Whenever I tell Dad that he is cute, Omar jumps up and down.

"He is not cute!" Omar yells. "Girls are cute. Dad is cool. Boys are cool, and Dad is a boy!"

"Dad is too old to be a boy!" I say.

"I know that!" Omar says. "Dad is a man, but men are like boys and they are cool."

"Yeah, yeah," I say. "Dad is a dude and he is cool."

Aisha always greets Dad, too. Aisha has brown eyes and brown hair. Her skin is white but her face is always a little red, especially when she rides her bike. She also likes to dress up her dolls. She and Omar play together all the time. They are so close, they act like they are twins! They team up whenever they have a problem, but they also fight about the smallest things.

After Dad arrives home, Aisha waits for him to head towards his bedroom. He always changes out of his work clothes when he gets home, but Aisha has a plan. This is her favorite part of the day because we play her favorite game.

"Get him!" she yells.

My Dad runs full speed toward the bedroom. Aisha, Omar and I chase him. One of us always catches him. Actually, he always lets us catch him. Aisha and Omar grab his feet while I jump on his back and swing around his neck. He has to carry us the rest of the way to his room. Then he throws us out! We wait by the door while he changes clothes. The second part of the game is about to start.

When he leaves the bedroom, he goes back to the living room. We stand there and let him pass by. Then we run up behind him and grab his clothes. All three of us pull back. He leans forward and struggles to keep going. He drags us along the carpet with every step. Then he calls out to Mama.

"Zainab, help me. Something is pulling me back!" he says.

He takes another few slow steps. Finally he stops.

"What is wrong with me? I cannot go one step further. It is like a monster is holding me!" he says.

When he reaches the living room, the game ends. We pull as hard as we can so the trip lasts longer. We enjoy it more that way!

When he finally gets to the living room, he is sweating. He catches his breath then turns around quickly. We are all giggling so hard we can barely breathe!

"Oh, you guys are the monster. I will beat you up!" he says.

We take off in different directions. He runs after us but of course he never captures anyone. After a few minutes, we all go back to the living room.

"Dad is a dude!" we cheer together.

"What about Mama?" he asks.

He wants to make sure she is included in the fun.

"Mom is a dudette," I tell him.

Dudette is the English way to show that the dude is a woman. But even this word is Arabic, and its meaning is funny, too!

"You mean your Mom is a bunch of worms," Dad says as he laughs.

Dudette in Arabic means many worms!

"At least I am only one worm!" Dad says.

Now, there are four things my Mom does not like: worms, mice, snakes, and pigs. So she joins our game.

"Hey, you guys, leave me out of this duding game!" she says.

"Dude means cool," Omar says.

"I do not like to be cool or cold. I like to be warm," Mom says.

"Your Mom likes to be worm," Dad says. He is always making jokes!

"And the plural of worm in Arabic is dudette. So Mom is dudette!" I say.

That ends the brainstorming game. We are five people in a happy family. I would call us a dude family but in Arabic I would have to say dudette. The Arabic word for family is feminine so I would have to use the feminine version. Phew!

That is a lot of thinking just to make a joke. I am thankful English words do not have all that feminine and masculine stuff.

But really, my family is cool. I am very lucky to have a brother and a sister. Omar is a lot of fun and really smart. He likes to build things with Legos and blocks while pretending he is a builder.

When he collects ladybugs from the backyard, he pretends he is a scientist. Aisha loves me because she always tries to copy the way I dress. I guess that means I am sort of a hero to her. Between my brother, my sister and my parents, I sure have a lot of love! Dad was right. Family really is the richest kind of wealth. I have been blessed with real treasures!

Chapter Five
Dear President Obama

My family does more than just play games together. Every Friday evening, we all go to the mosque. A mosque is a Muslim temple where we worship Allah. Our mosque is a big, tall building. On top is a minaret, which is a tall tower with a balcony. There is a playground outside for the kids. There is even a Girl Scout program! I am always happy when we go because I can think about one of my heroes, the Prophet Mohamed.

One day before we got to the mosque, we stopped at a red light. A woman sat on the corner holding a piece of cardboard. She has made a sign that read "I am hungry. I need food". She was very thin and looked tired. It was freezing cold outside that day, and she looked awfully cold, too.

My Dad rolled the window down to give her some quarters. He only opened the window a few inches so the heat would not escape from inside the car. When she took the coins, her hand shook from the cold. She stared at the quarters then blinked. Her face moved just enough to paint a small, sad smile.

Even though the inside of the car stayed warm, my insides froze. Words froze in my mouth, and my blood turned to ice in my veins. My Dad drove all the way to the mosque before I could warm up enough inside to speak.

As we got out of the car, I said, "I thought America was rich. Why is that lady having such a hard life?"

Dad placed one hand on my shoulder to cheer me up. His hand floated to my cheek and wiped away my tears. He looked into my eyes without saying anything. After a long minute, he finally took a deep breath.

"Ask your president," he said.

I, Assmaa A. Andulsi, know all about

President Obama. I voted for him! I cast my vote in Mrs. Coffey's class. That was the first adult thing I had ever done as an American citizen. Christa and I had talked about it at recess that day.

"I am very proud of myself. I voted for the first time," I said.

"But Mrs. Coffey said our votes are not going to be counted," Christa said.

"We wrote our votes on a piece of paper called a ballot. Then we put the ballots in a box. They will be counted," I said.

"We have to be at least eighteen years old before our votes can be counted," Christa said.

"I have a feeling that my vote will be counted," I said.

I was sure that was true. I did not know how my vote might be counted, but inside I just had a feeling it would happen. Christa did not believe that, so she teased me.

"Maybe an angel will pick up your ballot and drop it from the sky into the box at the place where adults vote," she said.

I thought about that. I really do believe in angels. They can change the way they look so you do not always know they are around.

When I think of them, I picture them being about my size. They of course have wings so they can fly wherever people need them to show up. They are kind of like imaginary friends. I talk to them all the time about different things. People cannot see angels but they can see us, all right!

Angels are around us all the time. Actually, every person has two angels that stay near them. The angel on the right records the good deeds we do every day. The angel on the left records whatever bad things we do. My Sunday school teacher told me that.

There are other kinds of angels, too. There must be thousands or millions of them. Maybe because they have to take care of so many things, there might be a zillion of them! Different angels are in charge of different things. I did not think my two angels would fly my ballot over to the voting place. They were busy doing their jobs. But there might be another angel in charge of elections.

I liked the idea of an election angel. What if an angel really did deliver my ballot? I asked myself again and again! Anything is possible. I, Assmaa A. Andulsi, believe in angels but I really did not know if there was an

election angel. I decided that the next time I
went to Sunday school, I would ask my teacher.

Sunday school is a lot of fun. The room
has a lot of posters of Arabic letters on the
walls. Other posters are in calligraphy, a fancy kind of writing that is very pretty. Those
posters have verses from a book that Allah
revealed to the Prophet Mohamed through the
angel Gabriel. We call that book the Qur'an.
The verses are so beautiful they are considered
to be art.

Up at the front of the room is a white
board. The teacher stands there to write down
the things we will learn each day. All the les-
sons are about my religion Islam. My Muslim
friends and I are always surprised by all the
wonderful things we learn at Sunday school.
Food is also served there. The pizza they bring
in is not very good. It tastes yucky like cardboard. But the biryani is very good. That dish
is made with chicken and hot spices. I love the
couscous there, too!

The best part about Sunday school is
being able to see my friends. Maha and Aya
are two of my best friends. Maha is skinny and
tall, and she wears glasses. Aya is chubby and

short. Both of them always say really funny things. Aya laughs so loudly that people keep their eyes on her when we are together.

The day I asked about the election angel, I did not have much time to talk to my friends. I was not thinking about the pretty posters on the wall or the Qur'an verses or the yummy food. I had only one thing on my mind. I marched right up to the Sunday school teacher.

"Teacher Ahmed, is there an election angel?" I asked.

Teacher Ahmed is tall and thin. He wears a white thawb, a long robe with a simple collar and a few buttons down to the waist. His beard is so long it bobs whenever he talks, and he always keeps candy in his pocket to hand out to the students. He always has an answer for my questions but when I asked him about the election angel, he had a question for me!

"Election angel? What do you mean Assmaa?" teacher Ahmed asked. He smiled and looked like he might be laughing a bit. The idea did sound a little strange, I guess, so I told him what I meant.

"It would be an angel who can carry my voting ballot to the polls, so it will be counted," I said.

"Hmm," he said.

He paused for a moment while he thought about angels and ballots and voting.

"Honestly, I am not aware of such a thing," he said.

"Does that mean there is no election angel?" I asked.

"Perhaps there is. Who knows?" he said.

That was not a very good answer. The answer did not tell me yes or no. I sat there in the class that day thinking about election angels. Every time I looked at the posters with their beautiful verses, I wondered again. So the minute my parents picked me up, I asked them the same thing.

"Would an angel take my voting ballot to the place where votes are counted?" I asked.

"Why do you want to know?" my Dad asked.

"I want to know if the vote I cast in class will be counted," I said.

"Well, I am not sure," he said.

"What about you, Mom? Do you know if there is an election angel?" I asked.

"No, I do not know. I suppose there could be, though," she said.

Even Mom and Dad were not sure! At the
same time, no one had said it was impossible.
So every night I said a special prayer. I asked
that the election angel take my letter to the
ballot box where it would be counted. I did
not have any proof that it would work, but I,
Assmaa A. Andulsi, was happy anyway. If an
election angel would take my vote to be counted then maybe I could ask that angel for something else.

You see, I had a very special plan in
mind. I wanted to write a letter to President
Obama. I would tell him about my vote, of
course. I also wanted to ask him for a favor.
I worked on that letter for many days and
nights. Each word had to be chosen very, very
carefully. I changed from one kind of pen to
another so my handwriting would be at its
best. I even wrote on different kinds of paper
until I found a really good one. This was not a
normal letter. This would be read by the president, so it had to be special!

"How many chances in my life would I,
Assmaa A. Andulsi, have to write a letter to a
president?" I asked myself. "Especially a president I like. Especially a president I voted for!"

Finally the letter was finished. I read it

ten times to make sure everything was perfect.

Dear President Obama,

I voted for you.

I am only eight years old but I hope they will count my ballot. I sent it with the election angel. I watched the election and when they announced you as the winner, I knew my ballot had been counted. The election angel did not let me down.

Now I am sending this letter with him. I know you will receive it. I want to ask you for one favor. Maybe it is not a favor since you are supposed to help all Americans but I will still call it a favor.

I saw a woman standing on the corner. She had no place to live and no food to eat. My Dad gave her some money. It was so cold that day the woman's hands shook. I worry about her all the time. I do not know why her life is so hard when America is so rich.

Mr. President, all I want is your promise that you will do something to change the life of this woman. Help her get enough money so she can find a place to live and buy food and warm clothes.

Thank you,
Assmaa A. Andulsi
Riverside, California

The letter was as perfect as I, Assmaa A. Andulsi, could make it. I carefully folded the paper and sealed it inside an envelope. I wrote my return address on the corner. My parents helped me look up the address for the White House online. I wrote the president's address in the middle and put a stamp on the envelope. My favor was ready to fly out on the wings of the special angel.

Chapter Six
Class Class!!

I, Assmaa A. Andulsi, felt really special after writing a letter to the president. Not a single one of my friends had ever written a letter to the leader of our country! At least, at that point they had not. But that was about to change. That special angel was about to become really busy hauling letters to the White House!

It all started one night when my family was playing games as usual. I, Assmaa A. Andulsi, had created a game called Class Class.

Well, actually my sister Aisha and I had made up the Class Class game. I do not remember exactly who started it first, but both of us added different ideas about how to play.

An Arabic saying claims that baby mice will know how to dig a hole no matter where they are raised. Now, my father is not a mouse, and my mother would never marry a mouse but Aisha and I learned how to create games from our Dad. And because we both worked on Class Class, that game is super fun!

If I had to say which one of us perfected the Class Class game then I would pick Aisha. She loves to be the teacher. It is her favorite job. It is like she was born to be a teacher, especially for Omar. Because Omar is the baby of our family, he loves to play with Aisha. After I wrote my letter to President Obama, I found them in the living room getting ready to play.

"Omar, our class will start at 5 o'clock. We will have recess at 6 o'clock," Aisha said.

"OK, teacher," Omar said.

"Class Class!" Aisha yelled proudly.

"Yes yes!" Omar said.

He is lucky because he is the only student in her class.

"Today we are going to talk about

swimming. Anybody like swimming?" Aisha asked.

"Me! Me! Me!" Omar said.

"Great, Omar. Swimming is cool," Aisha said.

Then she started the lesson.

"An elephant swims at the beach while an ant waits under a parasol. Anybody know why the ant waits for the elephant?" Aisha asked.

Omar raised both hands and yelled, "Me! Me, teacher!"

She acted as if she was picking him out of forty students.

"OK, Omar, you answer the question," Aisha said.

"Because the ant was the elephant's swimming teacher," Omar said.

"Nooo," Aisha said with a smile.

"Hmm. Maybe she was his babysitter. She waited for him to finish so she could take him home," Omar said.

"That is a smart idea, Omar. But it is not the correct answer," Aisha said.

"Hmm. Maybe she was a police officer. Maybe elephants were not allowed at the beach. So she was going to give him a ticket for swimming in the wrong place," Omar said.

"Very good answer but not the correct one," Aisha said.

"OK, I give up. I am not in this class anymore. I want to go play," Omar said.

"No, students! You can only play at recess. It is class time now," Aisha said firmly.

"I am tired of the elephant and ant story," Omar said.

"OK, I will tell you the answer. The ant was waiting for the elephant to be done so she could use his swimming suit," Aisha said.

They both laughed. Omar actually had tears in his eyes!

He likes most of the stories Aisha tells but only at first. When she repeats them over and over, he gets tired and runs away.

I, Assmaa A. Andulsi, like to watch Aisha playing the teacher character. I really enjoy Class Class when Mom or Dad are trapped into playing. After Dad got home that night, we played the monster game until he dragged us into the living room. Then he and Mom sat down to play Aisha's favorite game. I joined in and even Omar came back for another round.

"Class Class!" Aisha yelled.

"Class Class," my Dad repeated.

"No. You should not say that, Amer," Aisha said. She sounded just like a teacher!

"What should I say, teacher?" he asked with a childish voice.

"You have to say, 'Yes yes,'" Aisha said.

"OK, teacher. Please do not give me a bad mark," Dad said. He sounded like he was going to cry.

"OK. I am going to samhek this time. Do not do it again," she said.

"Samhek? What is that teacher? Are you talking Spanish to me?" Dad asked.

"No. Samhek is not Spanish. It is Arabic and it means to forgive," Aisha said patiently.

"OK. Sorry, Ms. Andulsi," Dad said.

"Class Class, our lesson today will be about water," Aisha said.

"Oh, this sounds fun," Mom said.

"Water is very important. People, animals and plants need water to live. Correct?" teacher Aisha asked.

"Correct, teacher!" the class shouted.

"Anyone know how much water is in our bodies?" Aisha asked with a sly smile.

"Me! Me! Me!" the students yelled. Aisha pointed to Omar.

"Three cups," he said.

"No. Much more than that," Aisha said with a laugh.

"Then how much is in the body?" Mom asked.

"Two-thirds of a body's weight is water. So if Omar weighs thirty pounds, twenty of those pounds are water," Aisha said.

"Wow. That is a lot!" Mama said.

Omar puffed out his cheeks and stuck his arms out to each side. He wobbled around as if all that water inside him was sloshing around.

"How about me, teacher? How much of my body is water?" Mama asked.

"Hmm. I have to figure it out," Aisha said.

Even though Aisha enjoyed being the teacher, she did not know how to divide numbers or work with fractions. She was still learning how to add and subtract small numbers. Actually, I had told her how much water Omar held inside. So it was hard for her to figure out how much water Mama held. Instead Teacher Aisha moved on to the next question.

"Do you know how much water is on Mother Earth?" she asked.

Both of Omar's hands shot up. "Hundreds!" he said.

"Hundreds of what?" Aisha asked.

"Of water," Omar said.

"No!" Aisha said as she laughed.

"Thousands? Hundreds of thousands? Maybe zillions. Yeah, zillions!" he said.

"Two-thirds of earth is water," Aisha said.

"Wow!" Papa and Mama said at the same time.

Aisha had taught us everything she knew about water, so it was time for class to end. At the end of all her classes, she gave us a riddle. That night she had a great one.

"A cat falls inside a well. How will she come out?" Aisha asked.

"She jumps really, really high," Omar said.

"She pulls herself up with a rope," Mama said.

"She climbs up a ladder," Papa said.

"Class Class. You are all wrong about how the cat will come out. The cat will come out wet!" Aisha said as she giggled.

Everybody laughed and ran outside to enjoy recess.

Chapter Seven
A Letter from the White House

After playing outside for a while, I went back in the house. Mom was in the kitchen chopping onions. She put the onions in the pan with the lamb meat and turned the heat down low. It would simmer for a while before it would be ready to eat.

"Mama, can we post my letter to President Obama?" I asked.

"Of course! We can walk down to the mailbox right now," she said.

Dad came back inside with Omar. When he heard what we were going to do, he said he wanted to go with us. Sending a letter to the leader of our country was too special to miss.

"I want to share this very important moment in your life," he said.

"Me, too!" Omar shouted.

Even Aisha tagged along. I led the way as we all marched down the driveway. I stood in front of the mailbox looking at the address for the White House. My family stood around me watching my every move. I opened the cover and slipped the envelope inside. When I closed the cover, I stepped back.

"OK. I hope that angel knows the letter is in the mail!" I said.

"Why would an angel care about your letter?" Omar asked.

As we walked back up the driveway, I told him all about the letter. He remembered seeing the homeless woman. He had felt bad for her, too. When I told him about the favor I asked from President Obama, Omar grabbed my hand.

"I want to help her, too! I want to write a letter to the president!" he said.

"Not tonight. It is time for dinner," Mama said.

I patted Omar's sweet face.

"Do not worry. Tomorrow when we play Class Class, I will help you write a letter to

Mister President," I said.

We went inside and sat down at the table. All through dinner, I kept looking at Omar and thinking about how he wanted to help that homeless woman. I wondered if other kids might also want to help. Then I had a great idea.

"Mama, Papa, do you think I should help the kids at my school write letters to the president?" I asked.

Both my parents stopped eating and leaned back. Their eyes grew wide as they looked at me. They seemed surprised and very happy.

"Assmaa, that is a great idea," Dad said.

"Be sure to get Mrs. Coffey's permission," Mama said.

"Yes. Remember what happened when you thought you were a real princess. You do not want to make a big fuss like that again while she is trying to teach," Dad said.

I looked down at my food and blushed.

"No, Papa, I do not want that to happen again," I said.

He reached across the table and patted my hand. He smiled and his eyes danced.

"I am proud of you, Assmaa. You are

always trying to help others," he said.

Mama nodded. We finished our meal and soon went to bed. I barely slept because I was so excited. When I did fall asleep, I dreamed about the election angel. He flew across the United States with a sack so stuffed with letters it was nearly as big as the spread of his wings!

The next day I could not wait to get to class. I ran down the hall and waved at my friends as I zoomed past. Christa could tell something was going on so she ran along beside me. We flew into the classroom. Mrs. Coffey was at her desk. I told her about the homeless woman and the letter. When she heard about my idea for everyone to ask for a favor from the president, she looked up at me.

"Wow, Assmaa, that is a great idea! Today we are going to learn about the White House, so this will be a perfect assignment!" she said.

Soon all the students had taken their seats. Mrs. Coffey started out right away talking about what happens after an election. She told us about the White House and the Oval Office, the room where the president does most of his work. She had pictures of that room. It really does have curved walls that form an oval!

"Now I will ask Assmaa to stand up and tell us about today's assignment," she said.

I gulped pretty hard. I had not known she was going to ask me to teach the class! I had been the teacher during our family's game of Class Class plenty of times, but standing in front of my family was one thing, leading a whole room full of students was another! I was nervous but I told everyone about the woman and the letter and the favor. When I was done, everyone cheered!

"This will be so cool!" Christa said.

"I never knew we could write a letter to the president," the boy next to her said.

"Anyone can write a letter to the president. It is one of your rights as an American citizens," Mrs. Coffey said.

Everyone took out their notebooks. The room grew very quiet as we wrote. The sound of all those pencils scratching away sounded just like the rustle of angel wings! Since I had already written my letter, Mrs. Coffey sent me to the supply room to get envelopes. I passed them out and wrote the address for the White House on the board. One by one, the students walked up to Mrs. Coffey's desk and set their letters on the corner. The stack was so tall it kept falling over!

After school, Mom picked me and Aisha up. All during the drive home, I kept seeing that big stack of letters to the president. The thought made me feel really warm in my heart. I had never felt that way before, not even when everyone thought I was a real princess and gave me flowers and took my picture!

And then, just two weeks later, I went home and found a very special letter waiting on the table. The envelope had a return address in blue ink that read The Office of the President. Mr. Obama had written me back!

Mama had called Papa to tell him, so he had taken a late lunch break so he could come home and watch me read the letter. My hands shook as I carefully opened the envelope. Inside was a piece of paper so thick I thought it was several stuck together! At the top, the banner said The White House, Washington.

This is what the letter said:

Dear Assmaa. A. Andulsi,
I was pleased to hear you are so
interested in this country that you voted for

me even though you are only eight years old. I was also pleased to know how much you want to help others who are less fortunate than you.

Your support and efforts are very greatly appreciated. I am aware of the issue of homelessness in America and am moving forward with efforts to help those people, too.

You are to be complemented for wanting so much to help others. Your efforts are in the best interests of all Americans.

Sincerely Yours,

President Barack Hussein Obama

At first I did not know what to say. I, Assmaa A. Andulsi, had gotten a letter from the president! Mama said we would have to put it someplace special. Papa said he would have it framed and we could hang it in my room. I just nodded and kept touching the paper. when I prayed to Allah that night, I sent out a big thank you to the election angel.

Then, the very next day, I was in for a bigger shock. I went to class and everyone there had also gotten a letter from the White House! Most kids had left theirs at home so the letters would not get torn or wrinkled.

Some had copies their parents had

printed out on their home computers. After Ms. Coffey read the copies, she held the letters up high.

"That is democracy at work. Even you young kids can be heard in the White House!" she said.

I knew that it was the work of democracy and the angel I had begged for help every night. I felt that warm feeling that comes whenever I help others. It was the best feeling...even better than having President Obama write me a letter!

Chapter Eight
Super-duper Ramadan

Writing the letter to the president and getting the class to write one was one way I helped other people. It is good to help other people, and people who help others are good. But you do not just get that way without trying. You have to work on being good every day. And even though I, Assmaa A. Andulsi, work on it every day, I still manage to get into trouble!

So, to help me be a good person, I look forward to a certain time of year. It is called Ramadan. I like it so much I call it super-duper Ramadan! My parents and I fast every year during that time. Fasting means we go without eating any food. Ramadan lasts thirty whole days! From the moment the sun rises to the time it sets, we do not eat or drink anything. The fast is one of the important parts of Islam and is called sawm, We do sawm so we can think about important spiritual things.

I, Assmaa A. Andulsi, fasted for the first time when I was only six years old. Mom and Dad always fast the entire day. When the sun finally sets, they break their fast and eat. For my first Ramadan, I was too young to go the whole day without eating. I also could not fast for thirty days. That is a really long time! So I fasted only during one day for only part of the day. Now that I am older, I fast for three half days. If I add up the three half days, that equals more than one day!

During Ramadan, I do everything else as usual. I still have to go to school and do homework at night. This year, though, I got into trouble. On the third and last day of my fast, I went to school. It was a Monday, and it was also Kevin Coffey's birthday. Kevin is really short and his hair is as soft as a baby's hair. He is kind of annoying and sometimes we argue. The arguments are over little things like whether a color is tan or brown. But I really like his Mom, Mrs. Coffey!

Since it was Kevin's birthday, Mrs. Coffey brought chocolate-chip ice cream cones and Oreo cookies to class. I, Assmaa A. Andulsi, love chocolate-chip ice cream and Oreo cookies! But I was fasting. I was not allowed to eat anything until later in the day. I could smell the Oreos and their creamy middles. The ice cream was already melting a little. That is when it tastes the best!

Mrs. Coffey had asked Ms. Hill to come help with the celebration. Ms. Hill had been my kindergarten teacher. She is very patient and wise. My first year at school, she made class so fun my Dad felt left out. Back when he went to school there had been no such thing as kindergarten. So he says if he ever has to take kindergarten, he will take it from Ms. Hill. I tell him that is silly. He would never fit in those tiny little chairs behind those tiny little desks!

Anyway, there I was so hungry because of the Ramadan fast on Kevin's birthday. Mrs. Coffey dished out the ice cream while Ms. Hill put a few cookies on a napkin. The students went up to the front of the room one at a time to get their treats. When it was my turn, I stayed seated in my chair.

"I cannot have any snacks right now," I said.

"Why, Assmaa, are you sick?" Mrs. Coffey asked.

"No. I am fasting today," I said.

"You are so skinny already you do not need to fast! Eat now and fast tomorrow," Ms. Hill said.

"I promised Allah I would fast today," I said.

I was still sitting at my desk but my eyes gobbled up the ice cream and cookies! All the other students had their snacks already so Mrs. Coffey made an ice cream cone for herself. She licked at the melting globs of ice cream before they ran down her hands.

"Yummy ice cream," she said.

Ms. Hill made a cone for herself and sang out, "Yummyyyy ice cream!"

I could not believe what I was seeing! My two favorite teachers were eating during Ramadan while the sun was still out! All these years I had thought they were both so wise and wonderful. I had looked up to them and listened to everything they said. Now they were doing something awful. They were not supposed to eat until after dark. I felt my face grow red and tears washed my cheeks. I was so angry!

"That is haraam!" I yelled.

Haraam means a bad deed. The angels who sat on my teachers' left shoulders were busy writing down their deeds!

"You are adults and have to fast for Ramadan!" I shouted.

All my classmates stopped crunching on their ice cream cones. Their faces turned pale with shock. I had yelled at two adults! And not just any adults but two teachers! Then I realized that Mrs. Coffey and Ms. Hill were laughing. The other students relaxed and kept eating.

"No, Assmaa, we are not fasting for Ramadan," Mrs. Coffey said.

"We have never fasted for Ramadan," Ms. Hill said.

"Then Allah will put both of you in the hell fire!" I yelled.

Again everybody stopped eating and laughing and talking. The room was so quiet I could hear my breath choke deep inside my throat. Mrs. Coffey and Ms. Hill whispered to each other. Then Ms. Hill threw the rest of her ice cream cone into the trash can.

"Assmaa, please go with Ms. Hill to the principal's office," Mrs. Coffey said.

I was in trouble, big trouble, huge trouble. Super-duper trouble! But why? Mrs. Coffey and Ms. Hill had done the bad deed, not me! But they were my teachers. Dad and Mom had told me to always obey them. So I followed Ms. Hill out into the hall.

Ms. Hill is very tall. She walked so quickly I had to rush to keep up. I was behind her the whole time. Her hair is really short so I could see the back of her neck. It was really red. That meant she was probably very angry with me! All the way to the principal's office, she did not say a word. She did that whenever she was mad, and I mean really mad. I, Assmaa A. Andulsi, was in real trouble!

The principal's office was connected to a room where her secretary sat behind a desk. Ms. Hill left the door open so I could look into Ms. Mumper's office. Pictures of her children and grandchildren were on the walls. A few pottery dishes she had made sat on her bookshelves. The awards she had received for being such a good principal shone in the overhead lights. Posters with happy sayings like Smile and the World Smiles With You hung everywhere. I tried to paste on a smile but it slid off my lips before my mouth could catch it.

Nobody talked to me, not even Ms. Ramirez. Usually she was pretty cool. She was tall and skinny, and her skin was the same tan color as mine. At the beginning of the school year, she had heard that I kept forgetting to bring pencils to class so she had given me a whole bag of pencils. Usually she made me laugh by telling me jokes but not that day! She just typed at the computer and did not talk to me.

Ms. Hill whispered to Mrs. Mumper for a long time. Mrs. Mumper nodded and looked at me. It was awfully quiet in that office. I was hoping she would say something, anything. I was afraid of the silence. It meant the trouble was bigger than giving a wrong answer. It was bigger than forgetting to do my homework. It was bigger than I could ever imagine!

"You, Assmaa A. Andulsi, are in a su-per-duper trouble," I whispered to myself.

"Assmaa, please sit on the chair outside my office door. I am going to ask your mother to come to school," Mrs. Mumper said.

Oh, boy, that really was some big trouble! I walked to the chair near the door. I was so scared I felt a little dizzy. I wondered if the angel on my left shoulder was writing all this down.

Chapter Nine
A Blue Day

After I waited for a while outside of the principal's office, Mom showed up. As she stepped into Ms. Ramirez's room, Mom looked at me but did not say anything. Whenever I made her mad, she would say "La howla wala quwata illa billah," which means oh God, help me. If she was really upset she might say, "Naharek Azrak Ya Assmaa," which meant O Assmaa, your day will be blue. She said that because having a blue day meant you were having a bad day.

She never raised her voice, though.

She always spoke softly. I dreaded those soft words because they meant she was super-duper angry. When she did not speak to me at all, that was the softest she could go. No words could describe how much trouble I was in!

She went into the office to talk to Ms. Mumper and Ms. Hill. They shut the door. I waited. The chair seemed very hard and I squirmed the whole time. As I thought about the super-duper trouble, I started crying again. Ms. Ramirez looked up from the keyboard. She did not say anything but she gave me a lovely smile, and a tissue to wipe my eyes. Somehow that made me feel better inside.

I remembered the things my father had told me about fasting. We gain so many blessings from fasting that they cannot be counted! Fasting provides more blessings than the candy kids gather on Halloween. There are more blessings than Christmas presents under a giant Christmas tree. There are more blessings than there are angels! I was still fasting. That was a good thing. A whisper deep in my heart said, Assmaa A. Andulsi, you will be in super-duper shape.

My Mom slammed the door to the principal's office. Her face did not move. I could not see any sign of the tiny smile she wore whenever she teased me. But the pinch around her eyes that showed up whenever she was angry was not there, either. I could not tell if she was mad, happy or sad. She sat next to me and leaned over to whisper in my ear.

"Assmaa, you are in deep trouble, you know that?" she asked.

"But not in super-duper trouble, right?" I asked.

She did not answer. Instead she began talking in a normal voice. She sounded very calm.

"Assmaa, you know that different people believe different things. They have different religions. Ms. Hill and Ms. Coffey are Christians. Christians do not have to fast for Ramadan."

"Really?" I asked.

I was so surprised! I, Assmaa A. Andulsi, had thought all people fasted for Ramadan. I had not known that only Muslims fasted during Ramadan. I had yelled at Mrs. Coffey and Ms. Hill but they had done nothing wrong. The angels on their left shoulders had not written down a thing. No wonder all the kids had stared at me!

"I am sorry, Mama, I am really sorry," I mumbled.

"You have to say how sorry you are to Ms. Mumper, Ms. Hill and Ms. Coffey. The biggest sorry is the one you owe Kevin for ruining his birthday," she said.

I, Assmaa A. Andulsi, had to be brave. I had to stand in front of all those people and tell them how sorry I was. I had made a big mistake, a huge mistake. It had been a super-duper mistake! The principal and the teachers accepted my apology. When I told Kevin I was sorry, he shook his head.

"I do not want you to say you are sorry," he said.

"But I have to. I made a mistake," I said.

"The only thing I want you to do is to eat an ice cream cone. It is yours so you should eat it," he said.

I nearly started crying again. I was fasting! I had promised Allah I would fast that day for Ramadan! Then I looked at the clock. It was already pass 1:00 p.m. That meant it was time for me to break my fast! I could enjoy the chocolate-chip ice cream cone and Oreo cookies. I could celebrate Kevin's super-duper birthday with him. My third and last Ramadan day ended with the best blessing of all...a smile from my friend Kevin.

As I nibbled at the cookies and licked the melting ice cream, I thought about the super-duper trouble I had caused. My mistake had happened because I had not known about other people's beliefs. We believe in different religions and so we live different ways. Some of us fast for Ramadan and some of us do not.

If I could be so confused because I did not know things about other people, other people must be just as confused about some of the things I do! I wondered if there was anything I could do to help others understand what my family does and what we believe.

I did not think about it too much just then, though. The ice cream and cookies were soooo good! Whenever a fast is broken, any kind of food tastes extra good. The hunger in my stomach made my tongue happy to lick the smooth ice cream. My teeth crunched those cookies as if the baker had won the top baking prize! I was so grateful for having enough food to eat.

I had only been hungry three days in a

row. I remembered the homeless woman and her sign reading I am hungry. I need food. She was hungry every day. She did not fast for Ramadan but she was forced to fast every day. So many people like her went hungry every day. I looked at the cookies on my desk. Three cookies were left. I wrapped them in the napkin and tucked them into my backpack. I would give them to the homeless woman the next time I saw her.

Chapter Ten
Imagination

I, Assmaa A. Andulsi, had wanted to give the cookies to the homeless woman right away, but by the time I got home that day I was not feeling well. Mom felt my forehead and said I had a fever. She would not take me to the street where we had seen the homeless woman. She said I had to lie down in bed right away.

Every time I get sick, I fall into the ocean of my imagination. The fever makes me think strange thoughts. Weird creatures come at me from different directions. They do not want to hurt me but they try to take my toys, my clothes, and other things from my room. They even slip through the walls and try to steal my bike from the yard!

I would hate for them to take any of my things. I love to ride my bike all over the neighborhood. I pedal so fast down the sidewalk I feel like I am flying! If the weird creatures took my bike, I could not fly anymore. I would be stuck at home while Aisha and Omar have all the fun on their bikes.

Some of the creatures that show up are aliens from different planets. They try to steal my clothes because they want to fool people into thinking they are human. They put on the shoes with heels to make themselves look taller. But the heels are mine! They make me look even taller and older than I am. The high heels are very important to me so I yell for the aliens to get their tentacles off my shoes!

Some of the weird creatures are really tiny. They have hooks for hands and try to take my toys. I have a whole bunch of stuffed animals. The stuffed horses, dogs and rabbits sit on shelves in my room. The tiny weird creatures stand on each other's shoulders so they can reach high on the shelves for the rabbits. They stab their gross hooks into the bunny tails and try to drag the rabbits onto the floor.

This time when I got sick, I asked my Dad to pile all the stuffed animals on the bed. They were practically like my family, so it was all right if they were in bed with me. But there were so many they would leave no room for me. Papa sat on the bed and tried to calm me down.

"All your stuff is in a safe haven," he says.

"But the creatures are trying to take my things!" I said.

"All the doors and windows are locked. Nobody can break through brick walls," he said.

"The monsters will!" I said.

"Monsters are not real, Assmaa," my Dad said.

"How about aliens, Papa?" I asked.

"Aliens do not exist," he said.

He sounded so sure! I began to relax a little. Then I remembered that not all people are good.

"How about bad guys, Baba?" I asked. Baba is the Arabic version of Papa.

"Use aby," my mother called from the doorway.

My Mom does not like me to use baba. Aby is the formal word for father, so she wants me to use that. It is just like the difference between the English words Dad or father. Even during serious talks, my Mom remembers that she is a teacher!

"Just say your duaa," Papa said.

Duaa means prayers. I, Assmaa A. Andulsi, say my duaa every night before I go to bed. It really does work! My duaa keeps bad stuff from taking over my thoughts...except when I am in the imagination mood with a fever..

"Sleep, Assmaa. Allah will keep the bad guys away," Dad said.

"Look, Papa! They are coming through the walls. They are strange like aliens, ugly like monsters, and scary like bad guys!" I said.

My mother came to my room. She looked all around to make sure that none of the creatures or aliens or bad guys had snuck into our house. The brick walls were still standing. The windows and the doors were locked. She even went outside to check on my bike. My toys, clothes and shoes were all in the right places.

When she came back in, she looked at me.

"I have told you not to change your clothes ten times a day. When you do that, you get sick and make my night a long one," she said.

I like to change clothes a lot. I match up different colors to see how they look. Sometimes I put on one outfit then try on every single pair of shoes I own. If I am not sure which one looks best, I put one shoe on one foot and a different shoe on the other foot. Then I switch from side to side looking in the mirror until I can decide. Sometimes I talk to myself in the mirror as if I were a princess!

I really like trying on different outfits. I like it so much you could call it one of my hobbies. I pretend to be a model and practice walking around like models do. The imagination mood that comes whenever I get sick is not a hobby!

"Look, Papa! The bad guys are climbing down from the roof!" I yelled.

I was so frightened. I really could see them! They were blurry like a bad video. They sneered at me.

"Assmaa, habibaty, trust me. Nobody is there," Papa said.

"They went into the attic!" I shouted.

"We do not have an attic!" Papa said.

"Open your mouth," Mama said firmly.

She set a thermometer under my tongue. After a minute, she checked the reading.

"Her temperature is more than 102. That is high! I have to give you medicine" Mama said.

"My high heels! The alien girl is stealing my high heels. Please stop her!" I cried.

"Your high heels or your high temperature?" Mama asked.

All the monsters and the aliens laughed. I was shivering and sweating. I felt lost in the rough waves of the imagination ocean. Gusts of wind blew up off the ocean and knocked against the window. Lightning made the house shake as if a witch had thrown a spell. Thunder roared like a hungry lion. I was so frightened I almost fainted.

As I began to fall off the bed, something held me up. Two arms kept me from drowning in that terrible ocean. My mother hugged me tightly and gave me medicine. Then I heard her voice in my ear. She was praying.

Five times a day Mama performs salat, a specific type of prayer. It is a Muslim ritual that happens at specific times every day. The prayers she whispered for me were different. They were duaa, prayers that ask for Allah's help. And they really worked! The aliens jumped into their spaceship and took off. The monsters dissolved into fog then were gone with a puff of Mama's breath. The bad guys could not run away fast enough!

"They are gone, Mama. You scared them away!" I shouted.

My Mom's prayers were very powerful. But the little alien girl was still in the room. She came over to the bed wearing my high heels.

"Bye, little human girl. See you next time you get sick!" she said.

Mama said one last prayer. With that, the alien girl ran away.

As Dad tucked me into bed, I thought about the homeless woman again. What would happen to her if she got sick? Maybe living on the street and being hungry all the time made her sick. Who would take care of her if she had no place to lie down? When I asked Dad, he and Mom both sat on the bed.

"There are places where homeless people can go. They are called shelters," Papa said.

"Because they shelter people?" I asked.

"Yes. Sometimes churches, temples and mosques will take people in for a night, too," Mama said.

"Just for a night?" I asked.

"I am afraid so," Dad said.

"What happens during the day? Do they have to go back to the street?" I asked.

"Yes," Mama said.

I was about to ask another question when Mom patted my cheek.

"Rest, Assmaa. We will talk more later. Right now you need to get better," she said.

And before I could say anything else, I fell fast asleep.

Chapter Eleven
A Hajj Story

The moment I woke up, I wanted to hear a story. Whenever I am sick, Dad tells me really long stories. I, Assmaa A. Andulsi, love listening to stories. The best are the ones Papa tells. I just cannot imagine growing up without them. He comes into my room almost every night to tell me a new one. Any time he has other things to do and cannot tell me a story, I have a really hard time falling asleep. It is especially hard to sleep with Omar next door crying out like a hungry bear, "I need a story. I just cannot sleep without a story!"

Some of Papa's stories are funny. Laughing makes me feel better, so he always tells me lots of funny tales when I am sick. When I start to feel better, he tells me adventure stories. The coolest thing about Daddy's stories is that he mixes imaginary tales with real stuff. Sometimes he starts with a simple thing that happened during the day. Before long he starts making up new things. It is kind of like he is writing a book about our lives!

Some of the stories he tells are totally true. The Hajj story is true, and he has told it many times. Hajj means pilgrimage, to take a trip to a sacred place. Every Muslim must make the Hajj at least once in their lives.

Dad planned well for his Hajj journey. He saved up enough money to buy a plane ticket to Saudi Arabia. He looked for a group to go with because the trip helps Muslims stay connected to each other. Mama helped out by doing a lot of shopping for the things he needed. Dad also went to the doctor for the shots he needed so he would stay healthy during the Hajj.

Then he went to Mecca. Mecca is a holy city. The moment Dad arrived, he put on a special outfit made of two pieces of white cloth. Then he walked seven times around the Kaaba, a special building that looks like a big black cube. He ran between two hills just like the Prophet Ibrahim's wife did when her son needed water. Then Papa drank from a well dug by the angel Gabriel called Zamzam!

Dad did a few more things while he was in Mecca. And he is not the only one. Every year several million people go there to do the same things. After Dad finished all his holy duties in Mecca, he went to Medina. The Prophet Mohamed is buried there. Papa visited the tomb and the mosque there.

The entire Hajj took almost a month. That was a long time for Mama and us kids to go without stories! When Dad came back home, he brought a lot of toys and gifts. He gave me and Aisha pretty pieces of jewelry, dolls that had tiny little headscarves, and traditional Arabic clothing. I could wear the traditional clothes and dress up my dolls to look exactly the same! Omar got a toy camel, a tiny motorcycle, and traditional clothes. Mom was really happy with her gifts. She got some fancy jewelry, perfume that smells really sweet, and of course some Arabic clothes.

So now you know all about Hajj. My version of the Hajj story is true through and through. When Dad tells the same story, he adds in really cool things to make it fun. When I started to feel better, he told me his version.

Once upon a time, a man dreamed that he went to Mecca. He woke up the next morning and packed some clothes in a bag. He added some food and water then kissed his wife and children goodbye. He walked and walked and walked until he reached the holy city of Mecca.

The man performed all the sacred duties of Hajj. When he was done, he started walking again. Soon he reached Medina and he visited the grave of the Prophet Mohamed. He had been gone a long time. It was time to return home to his family. First he went to the souk, an outdoor market. The vendors sold lots of toys, clothes and jewelry. He picked out special gifts for his wife and three children before he headed home. He walked and walked and walked until he reached his house. He knocked on the door.

"Who is it?" a little voice called.

"Papa!" the man said.

"Papa is at Hajj. Go away, stranger!" the

little voice said.

"I am Papa and I have returned from Hajj. I brought a lot of toys, clothes and jewelry," the man said.

"Did you bring my jewelry?" a woman called from behind the door.

"Did you bring my dolly?" an older girl's voice asked.

"Did you bring my camel toy?" a little boy asked.

The door flew open. A little girl jumped on the man. She hung around his neck and kissed his face and hands.

"I leally leally missed you, Papa!" she said in her little girl way.

Aisha was the little girl in the story. At first she did not like that in the story she said "leally leally" instead of "really, really." But Papa told different versions over and over. Every time he pretended it was a different man's Hajj until the very end. Then it always ended with "leally leally."

After a while, we all knew what he was up to. Every time he told the story after that, he had to be careful. As the last part of the story came along, he had to stand up. He would look around to make sure he could run away.

"Then the little girl said…" he would say.

Then he would stop! Aisha would crouch down and get ready to run after him.

"The little girl said…" he said again.

Then he stopped again! We all giggled because we knew what was going to happen.

"The little girl said, 'I leally leally missed you!'" he said.

As he says the last part, he runs away. Aisha is right behind him trying to catch him. The rest of us laugh and laugh!

After a while, Aisha figured out why Dad tells the story that way. It is his way of saying that she is Daddy's girl. She really likes that! Mama told us why Dad gives her that special honor.

"Everybody else asked for the gifts when he came home from Hajj. Aisha cared only about how much she had missed him," Mama said.

When Aisha heard that, a shiny smile popped out on her red face. From that day on, Aisha was always asking Papa to tell the Hajj story.

Chapter Twelve
The Snail Debate

The minute I got better, I jumped out
of bed and joined my family for breakfast. I
asked my parents to help me find the homeless
woman. I still had the Oreo cookies wrapped
up in the napkin and I wanted her to have
them. Aisha started teasing me right away.

"Do not worry about that woman. She
can find plenty of snails to eat!" she said.

I, Assmaa A. Andulsi, do not have anything to do with snails. I treat snails the same
way I treat all other animals, with respect.
Maybe I even give them a little bit more

respect because they are so gentle and peaceful. I do not eat snails, I do not torture snails, and I do not play with snails. Basically I do not do any business with snails!

Daddy and Aisha always argue about snails. Aisha likes to find snails in the backyard. She puts them in a jar with a little snail food. Then she takes them out one by one and gives them each a shower. When they are all clean, she holds them up by their shells.

"Now it is time for your exercise, little baby," she says.

"Aisha, stop messing with the snails!" Papa says.

"I am playing with them, Daddy," she says.

"That is not playing. That is called torturing," Papa says.

"Oh, no it is not! Boiling them in water and eating them with lemon juice is torture!" Aisha says.

She knows that Dad used to eat snails. Some people think they are really good but I would never eat a snail, not ever! Papa keeps telling Aisha to put the snails back in the yard.

"Aisha, let the snail go. I am sure his mother is looking for him. Maybe he missed school because of you," he says.

"Yeah, right! How about those snails you ate when you were kid? Were they going to school or playing on the beach?" Aisha asks.

I love it when Aisha gets frustrated. She changes into a different person. She grows very serious and very funny at the same time. She argues until the end. Aisha is a furious girl! Papa always tries to free the snails, and that day was no different.

"I can hear the little snail crying. Maybe he misses his Mom and he wants to play with his toys," Papa said.

"How come you did not hear the other snails crying when you threw them into boiling water?" she asked.

Aisha got really angry about that! Sparks flew out of her eyes and face. Papa sat down and patted her hand. He was really patient.

"Okay, Aisha. What you are doing now is haraam," he said.

Haraam means a bad deed. I had told the teachers they were doing something haraam when they ate during Ramadan by mistake. But Aisha really was doing something wrong.

"It is haraam to torture animals, especially these tiny, lovely creatures," Papa said.

"I think it is more haraam to throw them in boiling water then eat them with lemon on top," Aisha said.

Aisha always added the "lemon on top" part because she does not like lemon. For her, the lemon made my Dad's horrible mistake when he ate snails even worse. But since they argue about snails all the time, I think Dad's real mistake was telling us that he once ate snails!

Papa had told us about people in his hometown cooking and eating snails. He told us that story for a special reason. He wanted us to know that life had not been the same back then. He wanted us kids to appreciate all the stuff we have now. But Aisha liked playing with snails. She used the story to defend her hobby.

Actually, come to think of it, Papa had never said he had eaten snails. I also do not remember anything about the lemon on top. I guess those people were poor and had no food except what they could pick out of the dirt. Aisha had added to the story with made-up stuff. That means one day she will be a great storyteller! But I did not feel like playing her snail game that morning. I did not want to think that the homeless woman might have to eat snails or anything else that was dirty.

"Papa, Mama, I really want that woman to have my cookies," I said.

"We do not know where to find her. I do not think we can find her again," Mama said.

"What if she is still hungry? What about all the other people who do not have homes?" I asked.

"There are places they can go for hot meals," Papa said.

"And there are places they can go for canned food that is already cooked," Mama said.

"Really?" I asked.

I thought about that while we ate. I was lucky to have a place to sleep every night. My family had plenty of food, and my Mom was a great cook.

"Maybe I can take that woman some left-overs," I said.

"Habibaty, I do not know where to find that woman," Mama said gently.

"I could take the leftovers to the place that hands out food to the homeless people!" I said.

"Assmaa, you have a very good heart but those places do not take leftovers," Papa said.

I thought a while longer. Then I remembered that sometimes our school held special events. Every year the band members sold chocolate bars to raise money.

"What if I set up a special event at school to help feed the homeless people?" I asked.

Mama's eyes lit up.

"That is a great idea, Assmaa! You could collect canned food the students bring in. The places that hand out food always need more," she said.

"If every kid brings in one can, we could feed a lot of people!" I said.

"Some kids will bring in more than one can," Papa said.

"We can feed dozens of people!" I said.

That was how we came up with the idea for a food drive at school. Some kids would only bring in one can of food because that would be all their family could afford. Other kids would bring in two cans or maybe even a whole bag of food. In Islam the act of giving is called zakat. Instead of giving a set amount, everyone gives what they can afford. Every can and box would add to the whole, so every act of giving would be important!

Maybe, too, I could tell people about zakat. It is a very important part of my family's beliefs. If people knew just one little thing about us, maybe they could understand our religion better. I had felt so awful after telling my teachers they were doing something bad by not fasting on Ramadan. I, Assmaa A. Andulsi, could help others learn while also helping homeless people!

That warm feeling came back to my insides again. I could not wait to get to school and ask Ms. Mumper for permission!

Chapter Thirteen
Generation I

I, Assmaa A. Andulsi, went to the principal's office the next day. Christa wanted me to play with her during recess but I had something very important to ask Ms. Mumper. I waited in the chair outside her office until she called me inside.

"Yes, Assmaa? What do you want to talk to me about?" she asked.

I had thought all night long about what I would say. Ms. Mumper had a lot of things to do as the school's principal. Asking for her help with a canned food drive meant more work for her. So I had to prove that all the hard work would be worthwhile. In the middle of the night, I had realized that the food drive would help both the homeless people and the students!

"My social studies project was about people my age," I said.

"Do you mean your generation?" Ms. Mumper asked.

"Yes. We learned that the oldest group of people in America is called Boomers. The next oldest is Generation X, and the ones like Mrs. Coffey are Generation Y. We had to come up with a name for kids our age," I said.

"What did you decide?" she asked.

"Well, we were supposed to ask our brothers and sisters about it, too. Omar said we should call ourselves the I Generation because he likes ice cream," I said.

"That was a great suggestion!" Ms. Mumper said.

"I thought so, too. But not because of the ice cream. I thought the I was for the iPhone, iTunes, the iPod, the iPad, and also the internet," I said.

"That certainly fits," she said.

"Aisha thought that Generation Z would work because it comes after Y. But since that is the last letter in the alphabet, what will we call our kids?" I said.

"This certainly was a tough question," Mrs. Mumper said.

"Papa liked I Generation the best. He said it fits because we are always saying I, I, I...I need, I want, I was like," I said.

"He does have a point," she said with a tiny smile.

"I didn't like that at all. I want to prove that our generation is not all about I," I said.

"How will you do that?" Ms. Mumper asked.

I told her about the homeless woman at the stoplight. I told her about the cardboard sign that had read I am hungry. I need food. I told her about the cookies I had saved from Kevin Coffey's birthday celebration. I even told her about being sick and how much I had worried about what would happen if the homeless woman got sick. Then I told her the idea for the canned food drive.

"Assmaa A. Andulsi, that is a great idea!" Ms. Mumper said.

"Really?" I asked.

I was so happy she liked the idea. I was also pretty relieved. I had been so worried about the homeless woman and other hungry people. Now I could help them!

"You can make the announcement every morning over the school's PA," she said.

"I am sure Christa will volunteer to help. And maybe Kevin, too!" I said.

"Tell students to bring their cans to the office. Mrs. Ramirez will collect everything in boxes," Ms. Mumper said.

I was so excited I jumped up out of my chair. I ran around behind the desk and gave Ms. Mumper a big hug.

"You are the best principal ever!" I said.

She just smiled and said I had better get going. Recess was almost over and I did not want to be late to class. I flew back down the hall. I felt so good! For the rest of the day, I felt like angels had picked me up and were carrying me around.

The next morning I made the first announcement. Several students wanted to help. We made posters telling kids where to drop off their cans and taped them all over the school. I could hardly wait until the food drive started. The whole weekend seemed so long!

Monday morning I dropped off Aisha at her classroom, then ran down to the principal's office. Mrs. Ramirez sat at her desk. A bunch of cardboard boxes were lined up against the walls. The minute she saw me, she gave me a big smile.

"Good morning, Assmaa. We have already received our first donation!" she said.

I looked in the box closest to the door. Five cans of food were inside! I ran to my classroom so I would not be late. At lunchtime, Christa and I ate very quickly. Then we met the rest of the volunteers outside the principal's office. Two whole boxes had already been filled and a third box was half full!

We lined up all the cans on the floor to sort them. Fruits went into one box while vegetables went into another. Boxes of dried food like mashed potatoes and pasta went into paper grocery bags. Every day at lunch we returned to sort the morning's donations. Soon we had so many boxes we had to move everything into the teachers' break room! Kevin brought in an old wagon for that. We loaded the boxes onto the wagon then pulled everything down the hall to the break room.

"Today one kid brought in two whole bags of food!" Kevin said.

"That is a lot of food from one family. Most kids are only bringing in a single can," Christa said.

"My family follows something called zakat," I said.

"A cat?" Kevin asked.

"No, silly! Zakat. It is an Arabic word. It is about giving. Everyone gives what they can afford. So a single can of food from a family that can only afford to give a little is as important as a whole bag of food from a family that can afford to give more," I said.

"Wow, that is cool!" Kevin said.

"So when I give a dollar at church and my Dad gives ten dollars, my dollar is just as important as his ten dollars?" Christa asked.

"Yep," I said.

"That is cool!" she said.

By the middle of the week, the newspaper had run an article about the food drive. The very next day, trucks started pulling into the school parking lot. The drivers were from different businesses in town. They each brought in a full box or several bags of food. One even brought in crates of apples, potatoes, and other food that would keep for a long time. This was turning into the best food drive ever!

Chapter Fourteen
Found and Lost

On Friday, my Mom and Omar showed up after school to help sort the cans and boxes and crates. I picked up Aisha from her classroom then went out to the van to help carry in empty boxes Mom had picked up at the grocery store. A few other people were in the parking lot, and all of them were carrying boxes or bags of food toward the school.

I saw someone I recognized. He is the imam, the leader of the mosque where my family goes. His job is to help people just like a priest helps people who go to his church. Imam Habib has a white beard that is not too long or too short but he does not have much hair on top of his head. He must have gotten donations from everyone at the mosque because he was pushing a huge cart piled high with boxes of food!

I was going to tell Mom I had seen Imam Habib. Before I could, Aisha threw all her boxes down.

"Aisha! Do not toss the boxes on the ground!" Mom said.

"Look what I found!" Aisha said.

She bent over and picked up something. When she waved it in the air, I saw that it was money. And not just any money. It was a hundred-dollar bill!

"I am rich! I am rich!" Aisha yelled.

I, Assmaa A. Andulsi, never find money on the street. Well, I have never found paper money. I have found coins many times, mostly pennies, but I never pick them up. Mom says they are dirty because they have been lying in the street. So I never touch any of them.

Aisha is always the one who finds money, I mean real money, paper bills. Most of the time she finds a dollar here or there. One time she found a five-dollar bill lying in the grass. Now she had found a hundred-dollar bill! I looked very closely. I thought maybe it was play money. But yes, it was real! It was a large, green, smiley hundred-dollar bill.

"Let me see it," Mama said.

We all waited while she turned the bill over and over.

"Oh yes, it is a hundred-dollar bill," she said.

"A hundred? A hundred dollars. Wow, that is a lot of money. I really am rich!" Aisha said.

She was so excited she jumped and bounced.

"A hundred? A hundred dollars. Wow, that is a lot of money. We really are rich!" Omar said.

He jumped even higher than Aisha.

I noticed that Omar had changed the "I" Aisha had said to "we." Very soon he would ask to buy ice cream with that money. Mama did not say anything. I guess she was waiting for me to say something. I kept silent. I guess I was waiting for Mama to say something. Finally Mama broke the silence. She stopped the dreams Aisha and Omar were piling up in their heads on how to spend the money. They were shouting out all the stuff they wanted to buy.

"This is not your money, guys. Somebody dropped it. If you are very happy to find

it, he is for sure very sad to have lost it,"
Mama said.

Aisha got quiet. Omar looked at her and
then at Mama.

"We need to find the person who lost
this money and give it back to him," Mama
said.

"Give it back? No. It is my money. I
found it!" Aisha said.

Then she broke into tears.

"Yeah. It is our money and we will never
give it back. It is not fair!" Omar cried.

The piles of ice cream, chocolates and
toys were vanishing from their imagination.

"How are we going to find the person
who lost the money?" I asked.

"We can put up a sign that says we found
money," Mama said.

"What if five people contact us?" I
asked.

"We will ask them for clues about the
money they lost. We can ask how much money
or how many bills," she said.

"What if two people say they lost hundred-dollar bills?" I asked.

"We can ask them for more clues,"
Mama said.

"I do not like that idea. What if we take it to the lost and found box in the principal's office?" I said.

"That is a great idea, Assmaa. If nobody asks for the money, the school can use it to buy stuff for the students," she said.

"No. I found the money and I should keep it. Not the school," Aisha said.

"Aisha, it is not your money and you cannot keep it. Do you understand?" Mama asked. Mama started walking toward the school. We all ran after her. In the office, she handed the hundred-dollar bill to Ms. Ramirez and told her what had happened.

"Wow. Good job, Aisha. I am proud of you. You are really a good citizen," Ms. Ramirez said.

Aisha's tears disappeared. She was very happy to hear that. She smiled at Mama as if she was saying thank you.

"I guess we should call the money found then lost instead of lost and found," Omar said.

We all laughed, including Omar! Then we went down to the break room and sorted out the food. When we were nearly done, Mrs. Ramirez came into the room.

"I just got a call from one of the businesses. When they dropped off their food, they had meant to donate that hundred-dollar bill you found," she said.

"Really?" Aisha asked.

"Yes. They forgot all about it and are glad you found it. They want that money to be used to buy more food," Mrs. Ramirez said. We talked about what to do with the money. Mama looked at the cans and boxes.

"There is a lot of fruit and vegetables and some pasta and rice," she said.

"Should we use the money to buy more rice?" Aisha asked.

"People need protein, too," Mama said.

"Like meat," I said.

"So we should use the money to buy canned meat," I said.

"What if the people who get the food do not eat meat?" Mama asked.

"We could get nuts!" I said.

"Yeah! That is a great idea!" Aisha said.

"Then we will buy bags of nuts," Mama said.

"And almond butter!" Omar shouted.

Almond butter was one of his favorite foods.

"Nuts and almond butter do not have to be cooked. That is very important when giving food to homeless people because they do not have a kitchen," I said.

We were all very happy because everyone who got the food would have healthy meals to eat. Mama and Omar went to the grocery store while Aisha and I kept sorting. By the time they got back, everything was done. Boxes were stacked high along every wall and covered every table. Mama added the bags of nuts to the pile and smiled at me.

"You have done a very good thing, Assmaa," she said.

That made me feel really warm inside!

Chapter Fifteen
Food Train

That night when we all got home, Papa met us at the door. He knew we were all tired and wanted to make sure we had fun after all that work sorting cans and stacking boxes. So he was ready to play the game we called Stations. I, Assmaa A. Andulsi, know how to play Stations. Actually, I was there when the game was invented!

Now, sometimes my Mom says, "Your Dad is always behind the trouble." That is true for the Stations game, too. My Dad invented Stations. But in this game, he has to deal with the trouble rather than my Mom. That is because he is the train. He gives us rides all around the house.

Nobody at our house can play the train better. Actually nobody in our house wants to be the train. Everybody wants to enjoy the ride! So, after our long afternoon sorting cans and boxes, he was ready to play!

"Woo-woo!" Papa cried.

Aisha, Omar and I were all ready to go at once!

"No, no, no. You guys need to line up. The train can only take one at a time," Papa said.

"What kind of train is that?" Aisha complained.

"Clickety-clack, clickety-clack!" Papa yelled.

He was warning us that it was time for the train to move on. We needed to hurry if we wanted to catch the ride. We lined up just like always with Omar first then Aisha, and finally I, Assmaa A. Andulsi. I usually go last because I am the biggest and I can wait more patiently than my younger siblings. I sometimes have a problem with that, though. I am still a child exactly like them. Why would two years give Aisha privileges I never enjoy? I do not know why but I got used to lining up that way. Omar jumped on my Dad's back first.

"Station number 2, please!" Omar shouted.

"Woo-woo!" cried the train.

As Dad moved around, he called out clickety-clack, clickety-clack over and over. The train can stop at one of nine stations. The main station is the sofa in the living room. We call that station number 1. Station number 2 is the dining room. That is Omar's favorite station because he eats his evening lomja, or snack, there. Station number 3 is the rocking chair in the family room. It is Aisha's favorite. Station number 4 is the library room. That is my favorite!

Station number 5 is the loft where we have the computer desk. Station number 6 is Aisha's and my bedroom. Station number 7 is Omar's bedroom. Station number 8 is the bathroom. The last station, number 9, was the most scary especially for Omar. If anybody asked for station number 9, he or she had to go to bed and go right to sleep, or at least pretend to sleep. The rules are the rules. The first time Omar called out station 9, he found out the hard way!

"When you play a game you have to accept the rules," Papa said firmly.

"Okay but I do not want station 9. Take me to station 1!" Omar said.

"You cannot change your mind when you lose or you make the wrong choice," Papa said seriously.

That was just like turning in that money Aisha found. The rules are the rules, and the rules said that good people did not keep things that did not belong to them. Because Aisha had done the right thing, the homeless and hungry people would get even more food. I did not always like following rules like standing last in line but I knew it was for the best!

The next day was Saturday. I, Assmaa A. Andulsi, usually get up pretty early on the weekends. I have friends to meet and things to do! On this Saturday morning, I got up even earlier than usual. It was time to take the donations from the school to the food bank!

My whole family pitched in. When we got to the school, five other vans and a pickup truck followed us into the lot. My Mom parked at the curb by the front door where the buses stopped. All the other cars parked on the curb behind her. It looked like a train made of vans with a truck for a caboose! I laughed because we had played Stations just the night before.

Now we were heading up a different kind of train!

The fifth van in line was old and blue. I recognized it from the mosque. Sister Fatima got out of the driver's side and waved. She is the mosque administrator and takes care of a lot of things that need to be done so everything runs smoothly. She is black and very tall with a large build. She offers her smile to everyone! No matter what kind of event the mosque plans, Sister Fatima comes to nearly every single one. It was so special to see her at the food drive!

The kids who had helped all week long with the food drive got out with their families. A whole crowd of people poured into the teacher's break room. We used Kevin's wagon and trollies from the cafeteria to wheel all the boxes and bags out to the cars. By the time we were done, all seven cars were stuffed up to their roofs! We even stored bags on the floors between the seats.

Somehow everyone squeezed back into their cars and we headed out. As we turned onto the street in front of the school, I looked back at the cars trailing behind. I remembered that awful day when I had lost

Aisha after school. I remembered my prayer and how quickly it had been answered. And there behind me was proof that my other prayer had also been answered. The angel had taken my letter to the president and had delivered it straight to heaven!

"There is no god but Allah," I whispered.

That is part of my family's beliefs, too. It is called shahada, when we say that we believe. Mama heard me. She turned to me with that gentle smile on her lips. Her eyes were shiny like she might be crying a little. I knew they were happy tears. She was happy because she was proud of me for helping so many other people. I was crying a little too because I was also very happy. I thought of that homeless woman and all the other people who would no longer be hungry.

"Oh, Allah, thank you! Thank you!" I whispered.

Mom turned into the parking lot of the food bank. A lot of people stood around out front. Near the curb were two funny looking vans. One was white with a satellite dish on top. The other was black and had a huge camera mounted on the roof. They were from the local news channels. The minute I got out of the car, the reporters rushed over. They wanted to interview me!

I, Assmaa A. Andulsi, was very glad I had picked a pretty outfit to wear that day. I was glad that my clothes and my hair were neat and clean. Not because I wanted to look good on television. I learned that lesson when I thought I was a princess! I was glad because I wanted everyone who watched the news to pay attention. If my clothes were baggy or my hair was messy, they might not pay attention. But because I was neat and clean, they would hear about the homeless people. Then they would want to help, too!

I was a little nervous, of course. Boy, those reporters were noisy! I was very polite and waited for them to ask questions before I said anything. My Mom stood at the edge of the crowd with Papa. They were both smiling so big their faces looked like nothing but teeth!

"How did you come up with the idea for the food drive?" one reporter asked.

"My parents helped me," I said.

I waved for them to come over. My Mom patted her headscarf to make sure it was on right. As Dad stepped forward, he put one hand on my shoulder and smiled at the reporter.

"Assmaa did all the hard work," he said.

"Other kids helped. You should talk to them too," I said.

I pointed at Kevin and Christa. Kevin pulled the wagon loaded with boxes over to where we stood. Christa seemed kind of shy about the cameras but came over with him. The other kids who had sorted food all week stepped up and we answered all their questions. I was surprised to hear them repeat things I had said.

"Some kids brought in a single can of food while others brought in whole bags," Kevin said.

"But that is okay. Every can and box is as important as the next," Christa said.

"Yeah. Everyone gave what they can afford," Kevin said.

"That is called zakat," Christa said.

She looked at me to make sure she had pronounced the Arabic word properly. I smiled at her and nodded. She turned back to the camera with a big grin. She did not seem shy anymore!

"Sometimes adults think kids are selfish,

but this proves we are not," Kevin said.

"You certainly have done something special here," the reporter said.

As the reporters wrote their notes and took pictures and talked into the cameras, we got back to work. We unloaded box after box and bag after bag. The people who ran the food bank helped take everything inside. We filled up shelf after shelf!

There was so much food we had to put the boxes and bags on the floor. Each box and bag was weighed before it was stacked up. After the final bag was weighed, the total was announced.

"One thousand, eight hundred and twenty-seven pounds," the food bank manager said.

"That is nearly a ton of food!" I said.

I, Assmaa A. Andulsi, and the other students and their families had done a very good thing. A lot of people would eat because of our work. In fact, people had already lined up outside to receive some of the boxes and bags. As I looked down the long line, I spotted the homeless woman I had seen at the stoplight. I never had given her the cookies from the birthday party. Today she would get a whole lot more.

Just then she looked up at me. She nodded just once as if to say thank you. She was actually smiling! I waved and smiled back. Then I looked around at all the people who had helped. Everyone was smiling and laughing. I knew they all felt warm inside too. The fact that I am a girl who is like no other did not matter. We were all the same. We cared about each other. We even cared about people we did not know. We had all worked very hard to make sure that everyone had what they needed.

At times in school, other kids do not understand the things I do. And sometimes I do not understand the things they do! Being different can cause trouble...super-duper trouble! Being different is also really cool. We all come from different backgrounds. We all have our own beliefs and ways to live. That means we are all special in our own way. And on the day we delivered nearly a ton of food to homeless people, we were all princes and princesses!

Right before we left the food bank, Christa came up to me again.

"Assmaa A. Andulsi, you really are a girl like no other!" she said.

I just smiled.

A Special Note from the Author

At the beginning of this book, you learned that this story is based on a real girl. Some of the things in this book really happened. Some of the things have been made up to keep the story interesting and exciting.

Assmaa A. Andulsi lives in my space. She is real! I do not remember exactly the first time I saw her. Maybe it was in the hospital where she was born with a bouquet of hair. Maybe it was in the backyard watching her sister collect snails. Maybe it was at the weekend school as she struggled to write from right to left. Or maybe I spotted her in the park playing on her bike. But I can assure you I know this little girl very well. I have watched her grow up all the years of her life.

Assmaa A. Andulsi lives in two different worlds. Each world pushes her to one side or the other while she tries to pull the two of them together. Both of those worlds color her daily life and make her different and special. I hope Assmaa will keep having fun in her daily life and keep learning, interacting, and making her world a better place. Who knows? Maybe one day she will see some of her dreams come true!

I hope you have enjoyed reading about this real girl and the real things she has done. I will write many more stories about her and her family. I hope you enjoy reading them all! Perhaps you will write me and the real girl a letter telling us about things you have done. You can tell us real stories and even mix a little made-up stuff into them too! You can send us an email to assmaaaandulsi@gmail.com. I promise to read every letter. Perhaps I will be inspired to write your story!

The End

About the Author

Ali H. Chemkhi is a bilingual author and a first-generation Muslim American who lives in Southern California with his wife and four kids. Some of his previous publications include dozens of short stories and articles in the Arabic language.

Several of his short stories have won awards. He has taught different subjects at several universities in Southern California. He is also a frequent speaker at mosques, interfaith banquets and other community events. Although he has completed a novel in the Arabic language awaiting publishing, he is mostly interested in writing juvenile books in English.

His goal is to create dialogue and nurture mutual respect and cooperation between Muslims and non-Muslims Americans.

CPSIA information can be obtained
at www.ICGtesting.com
Printed in the USA
LVHW030550180820
663484LV00006B/454

9 781734 576078